Hunt the Sun Runner
NOVEL

Hunt the Sun Runner

Ryder Windham

LUCAS
BOOKS

SCHOLASTIC INC.

New York • Toronto • London • Auckland • Sydney
Mexico City • New Delhi • Hong Kong • Buenos Aires

ISBN 0-439-45879-X

12 11 10 9 8 7 6 5 4 3 2   2 3 4 5 6 7/0

Printed in the U.S.A.
First Scholastic printing, October 2002

Hunt the Sun Runner

CHAPTER ONE

"Any sign of the Nallastian freighter?" Captain Breakiron asked, searching the skies.

"No, sir," answered the helmsman of the Fondor Space Patrol ship, a twenty-five-meter-long vessel that was distinguished by its dual-flared radiator fins.

"Keep scanning," Breakiron ordered.

"Yes, sir."

From his seat on the bridge, Breakiron looked through the cockpit's main viewport to the surrounding starscape, searching for any telltale sign of the missing freighter. Seeing nothing but distant stars, Breakiron grimaced.

The hyperdrive-equipped freighter and its five member crew had been in transit from the distant planet Esseles. According to the Esseles Space port Authority, it had departed on schedule through the correct hyperspace vector. But when the freighter was late for its arrival at its base on Nallastia, an inhabited moon in the Fondor system, the Nallastians alerted the Fondor Space Patrol. Five hours later, Breakiron and his team were still searching.

What had interrupted the freighter's journey? Breakiron could imagine any number of bad things: engine or navicomputer failure, decompression, collision with an asteroid or another vessel, capture by pirates or slavers, mutiny... the list was endless. He swiveled in his command seat to face the remaining member of his small crew, the patrol ship's navigator. "You're certain we're looking in the right quadrant?"

"Yes, sir," replied the navigator. "That is, unless the freighter returned from Esseles by a different route through hyperspace."

"Nallastians aren't risk takers," Breakiron said dismissively. "They would have stuck to the established route so they could return to the Fondor system by way of the designated vector. They would never...Wait!"

Jumping at the captain's outburst, the navigator looked up from his console. "Sir?"

Breakiron pointed at the viewport. "Look there, below that star cluster. A dim sliver of light. It's moving."

The navigator and helmsman followed the captain's gaze and located the object.

"Is it the freighter?" Breakiron asked.

The navigator looked at a screen on his console and answered, "Unknown, sir. It's not appearing on our sensors."

"No reading at all?" Breakiron asked, keeping his eyes locked on the moving sliver.

"None, sir," replied the navigator. Anticipating the captain's next question, the navigator added, "All our systems are operational, but I'm getting a dead signal from our electrophoto receptors as well as the full-spectrum transceivers."

"Strange," Breakiron commented. "Any chance this unidentified object is jamming our sensor array?"

"Unknown, sir."

Breakiron turned to the helmsman. "What's our shield and weapons status?"

"Fully operational, sir."

"Then we're not out of this game yet," Breakiron said dryly. Aiming a finger at the navigator, he said, "Get a visual on the electrotelescope."

The navigator looked confused. "But, sir, the sensors aren't—"

"Use your eyes!" Breakiron snapped. "And adjust the scope manually."

The navigator peered into a recessed oval monitor and manipulated the electrotelescope's controls. It was frustrating work. The device was powerful enough to detect small freighters at distances of up to five light-minutes, but it was entirely dependent on data received by the sensor array. The navigator did his best.

"Well?" asked Breakiron.

"Sorry, sir," the navigator reported. "The object keeps traveling out of my viewer, and I can't focus on it."

Breakiron drummed his fingers on his seat's armrest. "It might be the missing freighter. We'd better check it out. Check our shields and move in."

As the patrol ship sped toward the unidentified object, it appeared to slowly grow and elongate within the frame of the bridge's viewport. The sliver became a thin stick, the stick became an oblong, the oblong transformed into a thick cylinder, and then the cylinder became...

A derelict starship.

It appeared to be about four hundred meters long, sixteen times the length of the Fondor Space Patrol ship, and it drifted at an odd angle across the airless void. Illuminated only by the light of the Fondor system's sun, the derelict's gray-metal hull was pocked by numerous small dents but otherwise appeared intact. At the stern, three tapered, swept-back wings were affixed to a single bulky sublight engine that was scarred by black scorch marks.

The helmsman gaped. "That is definitely not the Nallastian freighter."

"No kidding," Breakiron replied. "Still nothing from the sensors?"

The navigator shook his head. "According to the sensors, we should be looking at empty space."

"Then something must be wrong with our sensor

array," Breakiron said. Eyeing the cylindrical derelict, he inquired, "Either of you familiar with the design of this heap?"

"No, sir," answered the two crewmen in unison.

"The dents on the hull were probably caused by micrometeorites," Breakiron observed. "Looks like it's been adrift for a long, long time." He surveyed the derelict's stern and said, "There's a marking on that wing. Bring us in closer."

The helmsman matched the speed of the drifting derelict and maneuvered the patrol ship so they had a clear view of the wing through the viewport. The marking turned out to be an Icon, faded by many years of radiation exposure. The icon was a gold circle that was divided in half by a single white line.

Everyone in the Fondor system had heard of the story of the starship that bore the sign of the divided gold circle. There was a moment of silence in the patrol ship. The silence ended when the helmsman gasped, "The *Sun Runner*."

"It can't be," said the navigator. "The *Sun Runner* is just a legend."

"Every legend has an origin," Breakiron noted, his own voice a cautious whisper. "And we may very well be looking at the legend itself right now."

"You...you really think it's the *Sun Runner*?" the

navigator stammered. "I mean, if it is, it has to be what...three thousand years old?"

"More like four thousand," Breakiron corrected. "Deploy a salvage-claim buoy immediately."

The helmsman punched a button, and a torpedo-shaped buoy launched from the patrol ship and flew to the battered starship. The buoy extended its retractable manipulators, clamped onto the derelict's hull, and began blinking yellow and red lights in a steady alternating sequence.

"The buoy's secured," the helmsman said. "Should we send a transmission to notify space patrol head-quarters of our find?"

"We can't," Breakiron answered. "Not with our transceiver on the blink. And even if we could send a transmission, there's a good chance the Nallastians would intercept it, and then they'd accuse us of hunting the *Sun Runner* instead of trying to find their missing freighter. Fondor Space Patrol would never hear the end of it, and neither would we."

"Then what should we do, sir?" the helmsman asked. "I mean, if this *is* the *Sun Runner*, we can't just leave it out here."

Breakiron thought for a moment, then asked the navigator, "Can you establish the derelict's coordinates and current trajectory without the sensors?"

"Yes, sir."

"Do it," Breakiron ordered. "Then enter the data into Little Brother, and send him home."

Little Brother was the nickname that the crew had given to their vessel's Seeker, an orb-shaped messenger droid. Equipped with a scaled-down hyperdrive, the Seeker was designed to make a one way journey through hyperspace and deliver confidential information to a specific recipient. In Little Brother's case, the recipient would be the Director of Fondor Space Patrol.

It took the navigator fifty-five seconds to prepare and deploy Little Brother. Ejecting from the patrol ship via a pressurized hatch, the messenger droid quickly located the position of the Fondor system, then vanished into hyperspace.

"Since we're still in the Tapani sector, Little Brother will reach Fondor in about thirty-five minutes," the navigator reported with confidence.

"Good work," Captain Breakiron said. "Now, much as I hate to leave this relic, we must resume our search for the freighter. Take us out, helmsman."

The patrol ship began to move away from the derelict's stern, but it had not traveled far before it was struck by a sudden, bone-jarring jolt.

Captain Breakiron nearly fell out of his seat.

"What happened?" he shouted. "Did we hit something?"

Before the helmsman or navigator could answer, all of the bridge's lights blinked out. Then the helmsman exclaimed, "Captain! We've lost all power!"

Breakiron looked through the patrol ship's viewport. They were no longer moving away from the derelict.

They were headed straight for it!

CHAPTER TWO

The three spherical combat remotes hovered into a triangulated attack configuration, targeted Anakin Skywalker, and fired. With his eyes closed, Anakin counted off three shots and instinctively sensed the trajectory of each approaching projectile. He moved fast, tilting his head back and bringing up his lightsaber at a sharp angle. As one energy bolt whizzed past his ear and buried itself in the polarized wall of the droid hold, the other two bolts connected with his lightsaber. He slammed the bolts back at two of the remotes, then spun and brought up his lightsaber fast, cleaving through the third automaton. The shattered remotes clattered on the metal floor.

From the droid hold's hatch, Anakin heard his Master's voice ask, "Preparing for our mission to Fondor?"

Anakin opened his eyes, deactivated his lightsaber, and turned to see Obi-Wan Kenobi. The droid hold was located on the mid-deck of the Republic cruiser *Unitive*, a scarlet-colored, 117-meter-long diplomatic vessel that was traveling through hyperspace to the Fondor system. Behind Anakin, three astromech droids, two power droids, and a sanitation droid were braced against the wall. The astromechs rotated their domed heads to view the bearded man who had just entered the hold. Obi-Wan did not look pleased.

"Imagine my surprise, finding you here," Obi-Wan continued, "after I instructed you to go to your stateroom and meditate."

"I did meditate, Master," Anakin replied as he clipped his lightsaber to his belt. "But I was restless."

Obi-Wan sighed. "Well, now that you've stretched your limbs, perhaps you'd care to join me on the bridge. We're about to exit hyper-space."

"Yes, Master," Anakin said. He picked up his robe from where he'd placed it, on the flat top of one of the power droids, and took a step toward the hatch.

Obi-Wan held up a halting hand and glanced at the remains of the three remotes that were scattered across the floor. "But first," he said, "you may clean up your mess."

"But the sanitation droid can—"

"You didn't have to destroy the remotes, Anakin."

Anakin shrugged. With one hand, he made a sweeping gesture at the remotes' fused pieces, using the Force to make them rise from the floor. A moment later, the debris whipped through the air and neatly passed through a trash slot in the wall.

Obi-Wan raised his eyebrows at Anakin's handiwork, then commented, "If the sanitation droid develops an inferiority complex, it will be your fault."

"I can live with that," Anakin replied with a grin. He followed Obi-Wan out of the droid hold and into the mid-deck corridor. Heading for the lift that would carry them to the upper deck, Anakin said, "Master, have you any idea why the Jedi Council has sent us to Fondor?"

"You know as much as I," Obi-Wan replied as they entered the lift. "Our orders are to pick up Bultar Swan at Fondor Spaceport. I trust she'll fill us in from there."

The lift came to a stop, and the door hissed open. The Jedi exited into the cruiser's crew lounge, then walked down a corridor until they arrived behind the captain's seat on the *Unitive*'s bridge.

Captain Pietrangelo, like her crew, wore a crisp blue uniform and black leather boots. In front of the captain, two copilots operated the controls that were positioned under the main viewport, through which they could see the cruiser's progress through hyperspace.

Anakin squinted at the bright cascade that filled the viewport. As a child on the desert planet Tatooine, Anakin had often dreamed of the day he would journey through hyperspace, the dimension that allowed for travel at speeds faster than light.

He had left Tatooine when he was nine years old, half his life ago. Now eighteen, and with many interstellar missions behind him, he still gazed at hyperspace with a sense of wonder, as if it were a confirmation that good dreams could come true.

Anakin didn't even want to think about the other kind of dreams. He did not know whether he should tell Obi-Wan, but his recent efforts to meditate had been interrupted by disturbing visions of darkness and distorted memories. Anakin wished he could forget he had once been a slave.

Even more, he wished he knew if his mother was all right. The last time he had seen her, she was still a slave, owned by Watto the junk dealer on Tatooine. Before Anakin left her, he had promised he would become a Jedi and return to free her. Nine years later, he remained determined to keep that promise.

The *Unitive* shuddered slightly as it dropped out of hyperspace. Outside the viewport, light seemed to wash past the cruiser and dissolve into darkness, while distant stars presented themselves in apparently fixed positions across the ever-expanding cosmos.

They were in the Tapani sector of the Colonies region of the galaxy. The nearest and most brilliant star in view was the sun Fondor, which shared its name with the most heavily populated planet in the system. Completely industrialized ages ago, the planet was covered by factories and cooling towers, and was famed throughout the galaxy for its extensive orbital starship yards.

The *Unitive* angled toward Fondor Spaceport, which, like the yards, was suspended in planetary orbit. The spaceport was a sprawling affair of linked modular hangars and docking platforms, built up and modified many times over several hundred years. It was a busy location, with dozens of starships and shuttles landing and departing at any given time.

As the *Unitive* descended upon a wide docking platform, Anakin nodded toward the planet that loomed outside the viewport and commented, "Fondor looks peaceful enough from here."

"Looks are often deceiving," Obi-Wan replied.

* * *

"I'd welcome you to Fondor, but we're not staying," Bultar Swan said as she boarded the *Unitive*.

"Always a pleasure to see you too, Bultar," Obi-Wan responded wryly as he fell into step beside her and headed back to the cruiser's bridge.

Bultar Swan was a Jedi Knight, and, like Obi-Wan, she was human. She wore a pale aqua tunic under a dark leather cloak, and her lightsaber's polished hilt gleamed at her side. She asked, "Where is your Padawan?"

"Waiting on the bridge."

"I have heard he is strong with the Force."

Obi-Wan was cautious, even with other Jedi, of discussing the extent of Anakin's awesome powers. His own Master, the late Qui-Gon Jinn, had told the Jedi Council that he believed Anakin was the prophetic chosen one who would bring balance to the Force. Few beings beyond the members of the Council knew of Qui-Gon's assertion, and Obi-Wan thought it was best to keep it that way. If word leaked out that Anakin Skywalker had the potential to become one of the most powerful Jedi of all time, it would most certainly make him a target of those who opposed the Jedi.

"He still has much to learn," Obi-Wan replied truthfully.

"Then I hope he's a fast learner," said Bultar.

"And why is that?"

"Because we may need a great deal of strength if we're going to prevent a civil war."

CHAPTER THREE

"Have either of you ever heard of an ancient starship named the *Sun Runner*?" Bultar Swan asked.

"No," Obi-Wan answered. Anakin shook his head. The three Jedi were seated at the round table within the *Unitive*'s salon pod. After the brief layover at Fondor Spaceport, the Republic cruiser was once again soaring through hyperspace, its course established by a set of navigational coordinates that Bultar had given to the captain. Anakin could not enjoy the spectacle of hyperspace travel from where he was sitting because the salon pod—for security purposes—was without viewports.

"Four thousand years ago," Bultar began, "Fondor and most of its moons were already being exploited for their raw materials, but one moon escaped industrialization when it was purchased by a man who proclaimed himself the Margrave Octan."

"Octan?" Obi-Wan repeated. "As in the royal Octans of the Darpa sector?"

"The very same," Bultar confirmed. "The Margrave planned to terraform the moon, which he named Nallastia, after his wife, and establish a colony. To transport his family and 867 colonists, the Margrave commissioned a starship, a four hundred meter-long Corellia StarDrive Alpha-class heavy transport named the *Sun Runner*. According to legend, the ship also carried three power gems, said to be able to disrupt magnetic defense shields. It is believed that the Margrave's ancestors had obtained their wealth by using these power gems to overtake enemy ships and seize their property."

"You mean, the Octans were pirates?" Anakin asked.

"More or less," Bultar allowed. "Some historians believe the Margrave kept the power gems on the *Sun Runner*, but others believe he may have hidden them somewhere on Nallastia. In any event, a week after the *Sun Runner*'s arrival at Nallastia, Margrave Octan and his crew left their families and other colonists to make a supply run to the planet Mrlsst. But before it could reach Mrlsst, the *Sun Runner* vanished."

"Go on," Obi-Wan encouraged.

"There was a search, of course," Bultar continued, "but the ship and the three power gems— now known as the Lost Stars of Nallastia—were never found. The Margrave's family chose to remain on Nallastia, which is today covered with terraformed jungles. His descendants continue to rule there to this day. And for four millennia, the people of Nallastia and Fondor have searched for the starship, which could be identified by a marking of a divided golden circle. Incredibly, a derelict has turned up that matches the *Sun Runner*'s description. It was found yesterday, drifting through space, right here in the Tapani sector. We're heading for it now."

"Who found it?" Obi-Wan asked.

"At present, that's unclear," Bultar admitted. "But from my sources on Fondor as well as Nallastia, I've been able to piece together the following details. Yesterday, a Nallastian freighter failed to return from a trip to Esseles. Nallastian authorities contacted the Fondor Space Patrol, which sent a patrol ship to search for the freighter, starting in the area where it should have dropped out of hyperspace. But instead of finding the freighter, the patrol ship found the derelict that fit the *Sun Runner*'s profile. They tagged the derelict with a salvage buoy, then launched a message droid to give the derelict's trajectory coordinates to the Director of Space Patrol."

"Why use a message droid instead of their transceivers?" Obi-Wan inquired.

"It may have been their only option," Bultar replied. "The message noted that an unknown anomaly was interfering with sensors and transceiver frequencies."

"Perhaps it was caused by the three power

gems you mentioned," Anakin suggested. "The ones that the Margrave kept on the *Sun Runner*."

"*Might* have kept on the *Sun Runner*," Bultar corrected.

"If all these details are true," Obi-Wan said, "why is it unclear about who discovered the derelict? Sounds to me like it was the space patrol ship's find."

"I was getting to that," Bultar said. "At about the same time, the Director of Fondor Space Patrol received the message droid, Nallastian authorities intercepted a signal from a distress beacon in space. Evidently, the beacon came from the missing freighter and it had been deployed eight hours before the Space Patrol ship launched their message droid. The beacon was transmitting a message that the crew had found the *Sun Runner* and it also provided coordinate trajectory data. I compared that data with the message droid's and I extrapolated that the freighter would have crossed the derelict's path..." She looked to Anakin, waiting to see if he had been paying attention.

"Eight hours before the Space Patrol ship?" Anakin conjectured.

Bultar nodded. "Exactly. Further extrapolation indicates the derelict entered the Tapani sector by way of uncharted space, from Unknown Regions."

"There are numerous inhabited systems between the Unknown Regions and Fondor," Obi-Wan noted. "It strikes me as suspicious that no one reported the derelict until yesterday."

Anakin shook his head. "Forgive me, but I'm not sure I understand." Facing Bultar, he said, "You're telling us that the Nallastian freighter may have encountered the derelict first, then deployed a distress beacon. And because of the sensor-disrupting anomaly, the Nallastians did not get the signal until the beacon was beyond the influence of the anomaly?"

"It seems a logical possibility," Bultar allowed. "As does the notion that the derelict itself is generating the anomaly."

Obi-Wan asked, "After Fondor and Nallastia authorities received the derelict's coordinates, what happened next?"

"Fondor sent a salvage hauler, and Nallastia sent a rescue runner. The rescue runner arrived at the derelict first and the salvage hauler just minutes later. To the surprise of the salvagers, there was no sign of the patrol ship—the one that launched the message droid—or the salvage buoy. To sum things up, both Nallastia and Fondor claim the derelict and they have exchanged dangerous accusations of sabotage, theft, and abduction. Meanwhile, the freighter and the patrol ship are still missing."

Obi-Wan said, "If the derelict is indeed the *Sun Runner*, I can imagine that the Nallastians would want it because of its historic value, but why is Fondor so determined to make the claim?"

"I suspect Fondor wants to make money off of it," Bultar answered.

"And you truly believe both worlds are prepared to go to war over this?"

"Yes," Bultar said. "There is much animosity. The citizens of Fondor view the Nallastians as simple-minded nature lovers, and the Nallastians regard Fondor's population as the worst kind of industrialists, who would sooner level a forest than plant a tree. Nallastia sends food to Fondor in exchange for protection from the Fondor Space Patrol, but beyond that, they try to avoid each other."

"Until now," Anakin noted.

"True," Bultar said. "The Nallastians are in general a preservationist society—but they will fight to the death to preserve what is theirs. When I learned that the leaders of Fondor and Nallastia were readying armed ships to travel to the site of the derelict, I convinced the leaders they would be wise to allow the Jedi to negotiate the situation."

"How did you manage that?" Obi-Wan asked.

"I told them that if they could not resolve their differences, I would be forced to turn the entire matter over to the Galactic Senate. They knew if the Senate were involved, a resolution might take years."

"We're meeting the leaders at the derelict?" Anakin asked.

Bultar nodded. "Senator Rodd of Fondor and Margravine Quenelle of Nallastia are already waiting for us. All we have to do is figure out a compromise."

CHAPTER FOUR

"Over my dead body," snarled Margravine Quenelle, the ruler of Nallastia, as she smashed her fist on the table.

"That would be convenient," retorted Senator Rodd of Fondor as he leaned back in his chair and examined the shape of his fingernails.

They were seated at the round table in the *Unitive*'s salon pod, to which they had been ushered after their respective ships—the Fondor-based salvage hauler and the Nallastian rescue runner—had docked with the Republic cruiser. The three ships, linked by the *Unitive*'s docking ports, traveled at an apparently safe distance alongside the massive derelict.

Senator Rodd, like the two aides who bracketed him, wore a black uniform that bore an embroidered logo for the starship manufacturer Republic Sienar Systems. Margravine Quenelle and her two guards wore more colorful and exotic apparel. The Margravine's robes appeared to have been made primarily from the skins of large lizards. Bultar Swan was also seated at the salon pod's table. Obi-Wan stood a short distance behind Senator Rodd's chair, and Anakin was similarly positioned behind Margravine Quenelle. No one was smiling.

Bultar took a deep breath, then said, "If we may proceed beyond discussions of salvage rights, I believe we can reach a solution for all concerned."

"Oh, I'm concerned, all right," said Senator Rodd. "In approximately one hour and fifteen minutes, the *Sun Runner* will drift into the Rimma Trade Route, and we could lose our claim. I'm not going to allow such an important relic to be seized by pirates or snapped up by a Kuat Drive Yards salvager. The best plan is to let my team tow the *Sun Runner* straight back to Fondor."

"So you can transform it into a commercial facility?" Quenelle spat.

"I never said commercial facility," Rodd replied. "I said an amusement center. Think of it as an orbital museum of interstellar travel."

"As I said earlier," Quenelle grumbled, "over my dead body."

"Please be reasonable, Margravine," Rodd said, trying to remain calm. "I mean, you don't want the *Sun Runner* to be lost again, either. We can resolve the issue of ownership later."

"Ownership is not an issue," Quenelle interjected. "As the direct descendant of Margrave Octan, the *Sun Runner* is my property. You only want the *Sun Runner* because you believe it contains the Lost Stars of Nallastia. I assure you, you are wrong."

Rodd sneered. "If the legendary power gems are not on the *Sun Runner*, how do you explain the anomaly in the area that prevents us from using our sensors?"

"I cannot explain the anomaly," Quenelle answered. "But I know the gems are elsewhere. And as with the *Sun Runner*, you will never have them."

Bultar Swan placed her hands on the table and folded them. "The fact that you both agreed to negotiate suggests you desire a resolution instead of a conflict. Let us consider a mutual effort to—"

"Fondor claims the *Sun Runner*," Rodd interrupted.

The Margravine glared at the Senator and countered, "It is not yours to claim!"

Bultar Swan looked up from the table to Obi-Wan, and said, "We don't seem to be making progress."

Obi-Wan stepped away from behind Senator Rodd's seat and moved to the side of the table where he could face both Rodd and Quenelle. "We all must consider the facts objectively. A derelict emerges from out of nowhere, disrupts sensors and prevents transceiver communication, and may be involved with the disappearance of a Nallastian freighter and a space patrol ship. And despite all outward appearances, we don't know for a fact that the derelict *is* the *Sun Runner*. Is it possible that the missing ships are being hidden within the derelict?"

"You mean, in an internal hangar bay?" Senator Rodd asked.

Obi-Wan nodded. "The derelict is certainly large enough to contain the ships. Margravine, did the original *Sun Runner* have an internal hangar, perhaps shielded by retractable hull plating?"

"I regret that knowledge has been lost to time," Quenelle answered.

"In other words, you have no idea," Rodd sputtered. "But speaking of losing things to time, the derelict is only drifting closer to the Rimma Trade Route. I want to know, right now, this very minute—will the Jedi grant permission for Fondor to salvage it?"

Obi-Wan's gaze fell to the center of the round table. He said, "I sincerely believe that if time were not such a significant factor, Fondor and Nallastia could have easily resolved this matter without Jedi negotiators." He raised his eyes and let them travel from Quenelle to Rodd. "But given the circumstances and information presented, there really is only one logical course of action..."

It seemed that everyone in the room was holding his or her breath. Even Anakin, who had remained silent during the entire meeting, had no idea of what his Master was about to say. But before Obi-

Wan could issue his judgment, a sudden, lurching sound reverberated through the salon pod.

Then the lights went out, and there was total chaos.

CHAPTER FIVE

No one in the salon pod knew what had hit them. The moment that the lights went out, it felt as if an invisible hand had suddenly upended the entire cruiser and hurled it sideways across space. Inside the *Unitive*, anything that wasn't bolted down went flying. Obi-Wan and Anakin stumbled back and slammed against the walls. Bultar Swan, Margravine Quenelle, and the two Nallastian guards clung to the round table. Senator Rodd and his aides toppled out of their chairs. Then, just as suddenly, the *Unitive* stabilized and the emergency lights came on. Incredibly, no one appeared to be injured.

"What happened?" Rodd shouted as his aides pulled him up from the floor.

"It felt like we were sideswiped," said Bultar Swan.

Rodd shot a look at Quenelle and said, "Is this your doing? Some kind of trick to gain what you want?"

"I was about to ask you the same thing!" Quenelle answered indignantly.

Anakin pulled himself up next to the pod's sensor panel. The pod had been engineered to eject from the cruiser in emergency situations, and had it ejected, the sensors would have displayed the pod's position in relationship to the *Unitive*. But the sensors did not display any useful information because they were not working. At all.

"Looks like all systems are disabled," Anakin said. "Including communications. We can't even hail the bridge. Did the salon pod eject?"

Obi-Wan scrambled over to the main hatch and visually checked its bolts. Six rectangular yellow panels set around the hatch's frame indicated that the pod was still secured to the *Unitive*. Obi-Wan considered throwing the manual switch to eject, then decided against it.

A small octagonal shield was set in the center of the hatch. Obi-Wan slid back the shield to peer through a transparisteel window, which permitted a view into the docking tube that linked the salon pod with the *Unitive*. Within the docking tube, the *Unitive*'s captain was approaching the salon pod's hatch. She saw Obi-Wan through the small window and signaled him to open the hatch. He did.

"What happened?" Obi-Wan asked.

"The derelict's sublight engine fired, and then it veered out of its trajectory," Captain Pietrangelo reported. "At the same time, we suddenly had a shipwide power surge. It disabled most of our systems. Engines, sensors, and communications are down. We're adrift."

"You saw the derelict's engine fire?" Anakin asked, surprised.

"Yes, sir," replied the captain. "That thing was operational."

"We can only guess who's controlling it," Obi-Wan said. "Could you determine its new course?"

"It looked like it was angling for the Fondor system," Pietrangelo answered. "I tried to launch a message droid to warn Fondor Space Patrol, but I'm afraid the launch activators are fried."

"What's my salvage ship's status?" Senator Rodd asked sharply.

"Still locked on to one of our docking ports, as is the Margravine's rescue runner," the captain informed him. "But it seems all three ships were disabled."

Quenelle whirled on Rodd and fumed, "I suspect foul play, Senator. I would not be surprised to learn that your patrol ship's crew has seized the *Sun Runner!*"

Rodd retorted, "I was about to accuse your freighter crew of the same thing!"

"This is no time for accusations," Obi-Wan interjected. "Has it occurred to either of you that there could be disastrous consequences if the derelict reaches Fondor or Nallastia—especially if it crashes?"

Margravine Quenelle and Senator Rodd exchanged nervous glances. Collectively, there were more than a million beings on Fondor, Nallastia, and the orbital starship yards. Quenelle turned to the Jedi and implored, "What can we do?"

Bultar Swan said, "We don't know who is controlling the derelict's course, but we know they must be stopped. And if there are innocent captives on board, they must be rescued."

"But how?" Quenelle said. "We're stranded here!"

Rodd said, "Starfighters."

"What's that, Senator?" asked Obi-Wan.

"My salvage ship carries two starfighters," Rodd said. "A CloakShape Fighter and a Z-95 Headhunter. Since they weren't in use when the power surged, they won't be disabled. They might be used to catch up with the derelict."

Quenelle faced Obi-Wan and asked, "Can you stop the *Sun Runner* without destroying it?"

"We'll do our best," Obi-Wan said. "Now let's get to those starfighters!"

At this point, you must decide whether to continue reading this adventure, or to play your own adventure in the *Hunt the Sun Runner* Game Book.

To play your own adventure, turn to the first page of the Game Book and follow the directions you find there.

To continue reading this adventure, turn the page!

ANAKIN'S ADVENTURE: HUNT THE SUN RUNNER

CHAPTER SIX

The three Jedi led the representatives of Fondor and Nallastia out of the salon pod. They proceeded through the narrow corridors of the Republic cruiser until they reached the docking tube that was connected to Senator Rodd's salvage ship.

The docking tube's hatch was locked. Obi-Wan peered through the hatch's transparisteel window and saw the salvage ship's navigator on the other side. The navigator looked back, his expression suspicious.

Behind Obi-Wan, Senator Rodd cleared his throat and said, "My crew won't open the hatch unless I give them the all-clear. If you'll allow me..."

"That won't be necessary," Obi-Wan said as he gestured with his fingers to the navigator through the window. If the navigator was at all aware that his mind was being manipulated by the Jedi, he did not show any sign of protest. Instead, he smiled and reached for the hatch's locking bolt. There was a soft click, and the hatch swung open.

"Excuse me," Senator Rodd said with annoyance, pushing his way past Obi-Wan to be the first one through the hatch. "I'll show you the way to the starfighters."

Senator Rodd led the procession down a corridor that was lined with reflective metal, which acted like mirrors to make the closed environment feel more spacious. Anakin was at the end of the group, just behind Margravine Quenelle and her two guards. As Senator Rodd and his aides rounded a corner, the salvage ship's pilot stepped out of an open doorway to Anakin's right and bumped into Margravine Quenelle.

At the sight of the Margravine, her guards, and the other unfamiliar figures, the pilot's eyes went wide with surprise. He had not seen Senator Rodd, and did not know the Nallastians had been allowed on board. Without hesitation, the pilot reached for his holstered blaster pistol and drew it swiftly.

The pilot was surprised when the blaster suddenly vanished from his hand, leaving his fingers aimed at the Margravine. Somehow, the blaster had landed in the grasp of a young man who stood nearby. At first glance, the pilot had assumed the man was one of the Margravine's guards, but then he noticed the lightsaber that was clipped to the man's belt. His eyes traveled down the corridor to Bultar Swan and Obi-Wan, who had turned in response to the commotion.

"You're fast on the draw," Anakin said to the pilot. "But I'm faster." He gave the blaster a twirl on his finger.

Obi-Wan threw a stern look at Anakin, then fixed his gaze on the pilot and said, "We're with Senator

Rodd." Obi-Wan gestured with his fingers and added, "You don't have to worry about us."

The pilot blinked, then answered, "No. I don't have to worry about you. You're Jedi."

"Give the man his weapon, Padawan," commanded Obi-Wan.

"Yes, Master," Anakin replied as he turned to follow Obi-Wan and the others, leaving the pilot gaping in the corridor.

"Wait!" the pilot called after Anakin. "I...I thought you were going to return my blaster."

Anakin answered without breaking his stride, "Check your holster."

The pilot checked. The blaster was there, snapped tight against his hip.

The three Jedi walked behind the Margravine and her guards, following them around the corner to find Senator Rodd standing before an open hatch. Rodd asked, "Did something happen back there?"

"A member of your crew just tried to shoot me," Quenelle stated. "I would be dead now if the young Jedi had not intervened."

"Hear that?" Anakin whispered to Obi-Wan. "She's talking about me."

"You're a show-off and a braggart," Obi-Wan whispered back.

Senator Rodd was aghast. "No one was injured?"

"No," Bultar Swan interjected. "But let us not waste time with discussion. The starfighters?"

"This way," Rodd said, and ducked through the open hatch. He led the group into the salvage ship's pressurized docking bay. There, a starship engineer was trying to restore power to the bay's tractor-beam generator, while two Fondor Space Patrol pilots looked on. The generator was positioned between two starfighters. Even if the starfighters had not already been identified by Senator Rodd, Anakin would have immediately recognized them as a Kuat Systems Engineering CloakShape Fighter and Incom/Subpro Z-95 Headhunter.

Anakin's fingers began to itch. He could not help it. Although he'd spent the past eight years training to be a Jedi, he'd never managed to grow out of his boyish enthusiasm for high-speed vehicles. His initial interest had been with Podracers, but after his first flight in a chromium-finished Naboo N-1 with twin radial Nubian 221 sublight engines, he could not look at a starfighter without wanting to climb in and fly off.

"Are the starfighters prepared for launch?" Rodd asked one of the space patrol pilots.

"Yes, sir," the pilot answered.

Rodd offered a satisfied smile and said, "Then here are your orders—"

"Your pilots are not prepared for this mission," Obi-Wan interrupted. "We'll take over from here."

"But I thought..." Rodd began, but something about Obi-Wan's gaze made him decide it was best to stop talking.

Near the starfighters, there was a rack of four pressurized g-suits and matching helmets. Eyeing the g-suits, Obi-Wan observed, "It appears this limited selection has determined who will fly." He turned to Bultar Swan and said, "None of these g-suits is your size."

"Then I'll just have to stay here and make sure the diplomats don't assassinate each other," Bultar said.

While Bultar inspected the fighters, Obi-Wan and Anakin quickly removed their robes and slipped into the g-suits. Obi-Wan was about to put on a helmet when he said, "Because of the sensor-disrupting anomaly, we won't be able to communicate with our ships' transceivers when we reach the derelict. So it's important that you hear this now."

"Yes, Master?"

"No stunts and stay on my wing."

"Yes, Master," Anakin replied as he placed a helmet over his head.

"You're familiar with the CloakShape's controls?"

Anakin nodded. "You know I am, Master," he answered, his voice muffled by the helmet.

"Then I'll take the Headhunter," Obi-Wan said. "One more thing."

"Yes, Master?"

"May the Force be with you."

They scrambled into the starfighters and belted in. After activating their engines, Anakin followed Obi-Wan's Headhunter out of the salvage ship's docking bay and into space. From there, he looked back to see the bizarre configuration of the inter-locked salvage ship, Republic cruiser, and rescue runner. He hoped the respective crews would work together to restore power to their disabled ships.

The Fondor system was easily located without sensors, as its sun was one of the brightest bodies in the starscape. Squinting at the sun, Anakin sighted the tiny speck of light moving in the direction of Nallastia. He knew the speck was the derelict.

Obi-Wan saw it, too. He angled the Headhunter's nose after the distant speck. Anakin tailed the Headhunter's starboard wing, and both Jedi punched their sublight engines at the same time.

Despite the derelict's lead, it was no match for the acceleration power of the sublight engines that drove the two starfighters across space. Ninety-three seconds after blasting away from the salvage ship's docking bay, the two Jedi caught up with the derelict.

Matching the derelict's speed, Obi-Wan steered closer to investigate. Anakin followed his Master, and surveyed the derelict's surface for any sign of a concealed hangar. Much to his surprise, he saw a small black spot appear on the hull, in an area that had a moment earlier been pale gray. A split second later he realized the black spot was not a spot at all.

It was a missile silo. A missile launched, headed straight for Anakin.

Anakin broke formation, veering away from the Headhunter and sending the CloakShape into a tight roll to avoid the oncoming projectile. Anakin glanced out his cockpit canopy just in time to see the missile streak past the Headhunter.

Obi-Wan saw the missile go by, then pulled the Headhunter into a loop, steering it up after the missile's tail. The missile swerved hard to port, angling back after Anakin's rolling starfighter. Obi-Wan had not known until then that the missile was equipped with a guiding sensor, but he knew better than to let a missile out of his sight before it exploded. As the missile soared after the Cloak-Shape, Obi-Wan threw his controls hard to the side until the projectile was dead in the sights of his targeting scope.

Obi-Wan fired his laser cannons. The missile exploded into a glittering spray of light, and he steered through the debris.

Obi-Wan's gaze swept over the speeding derelict and surrounding space, searching for Anakin's starfighter. Unable to spot it, he attempted to get a wider view by putting some distance between himself and the derelict.

He never made it.

CHAPTER SEVEN

After seeing the missile narrowly miss Obi-Wan's starfighter, Anakin had assumed his Master would follow his rolling evasive maneuver. When he straightened out and couldn't see the Headhunter outside his cockpit canopy, Anakin was sure that Obi-Wan must have dropped down right behind the CloakShape, covering his tail. But as he wrapped around the derelict's circumference, waiting for the Headhunter to pass him and take the lead, Anakin realized he had lost Obi-Wan on the other side.

Anakin looped back, flying so close to the derelict that he could easily make out the CloakShape's shadow slipping over the its hull. When he wrapped around to the area where he had last seen Obi-Wan, his eyes caught sight of something that looked like a small cloud drifting across the stars. Flying closer, he saw that the cloud was made up of glittering bits of plasteel and durasteel.

"Master?" Anakin said out loud. His throat had gone dry. He could not see any large piece of wreckage that would indicate whether he was looking at the remains of a Z-95 Headhunter. Anakin felt a sudden rage swell within him, and the salty sting of tears in his eyes. He blinked back the tears, then took a deep breath. He tried to concentrate, wondering what his Master would do in this situation.

In that instant, Anakin knew. Obi-Wan would stay calm. That was how Obi-Wan stayed alive.

Obi-Wan was not dead.

Anakin propelled the CloakShape through the debris and angled back at the derelict. Punching the accelerator, he zoomed back past the area where he had seen the missile silo. Just as he spotted the black spot that was the open silo, something moved within the silo: A second missile was about to launch.

The CloakShape fighter was armed with dual laser cannons, four concussion missiles, and a single proton torpedo. Anakin was tempted to unload his entire arsenal down the silo's mouth, but he knew that would be imprudent.

He lined up the silo with his targeting scope, then fired two concussion missiles in quick succession, so that the second missile launched a fraction of a second after the first.

The first concussion missile slammed into the head of the projectile within the silo, and the second vanished into the explosion caused by its predecessor. Smoke and debris were still billowing out of the ruined silo as Anakin matched the derelict's speed and flew in low. Through his cockpit canopy, he surveyed the twisted debris that filled the silo's cylindrical interior. Despite the wreckage, the silo appeared to be Anakin's best route to infiltrate the derelict.

He landed on the hull of the *Sun Runner*, anchoring the starfighter a short distance from the smoldering silo. Anakin checked the seal between his helmet and g-suit, then popped his canopy. Climbing out of the CloakShape's cockpit, he lowered himself onto the derelict's hull. Anakin trusted that his boots' positive-grip soles would prevent him from drifting off into space. He stepped carefully toward the silo. He was about two meters shy of its scorched mouth when he felt something shift under his right boot.

It was a magnetic mine.

Anakin did not hesitate. He leaped for the silo, diving headfirst. The mine detonated behind him, sending a fine spray of dust and metal shards in all directions. Shielded by the silo's upper rim, Anakin caught hold of a metal pipe that was secured to the silo's concave wall. He righted himself, wrapped his legs around the pipe, and slid down, crashing through loose debris until he landed on the floor.

He was surrounded by darkness. He took a deep breath, then removed his lightsaber from his belt and activated it. The silo's interior was instantly illuminated by the blue glow of his weapon. He found a sealed metal hatch set within the concave wall and noticed that its pressure seal was cracked, possibly the result of the missile's destruction within the silo. If depressurization had been a concern for anything on the other side of the hatch, it no longer mattered.

Anakin drove his lightsaber through the crack in the hatch, made a broad circular cut, then deactivated his blade. He launched a powerful kick at the center of the hatch, breaking it away from the seal and creating a hole that was large enough for him to pass through. Still holding his deactivated lightsaber, he ducked through the hole.

He found himself in a high-ceilinged chamber that adjoined the silo. It was lit by yellow lumas, industrial glow rods commonly used in construction and mining operations, that lined the chamber's metal walls. An automated rack was positioned beside the silo's outer wall, and the rack was lined with eighteen missiles. Anakin was relieved that he had managed to destroy the silo before the remaining missiles could be deployed. He could see that the silo's reinforced wall had been the only thing that prevented eighteen missiles from exploding as well. Then he noticed a long, fresh crack that ran up the length of the wall beside the missile rack. He suspected that the crack was the result of the missile that had exploded within the silo, and he doubted that the wall could withstand a second explosion.

Anakin had no idea who had assembled this hidden arsenal, but the missiles offered a clue to their origin. Although they were unmarked, Anakin recognized them as sensor-guided projectile weapons produced by Arakyd Industries. The derelict may have come from the Unknown Regions of space, but the missiles most certainly did not.

Beyond the rack of missiles, the rough hewn wall framed a sealed metal door. The door was about two meters high and a half meter wide, and it was without any visible mechanisms for opening. Hoping to examine it more closely, Anakin stepped toward it.

Suddenly, the metal door slid sideways into the wall, and two droids leaped out. Both droids were humanoid, with durasteel heads that contained high-speed optic visors. Anakin recognized the droids as expensive Duelist Elites, which were used for fencing instruction. They were manufactured by Trang Robotics in the remote Almanian system, which was on the other side of the charted galaxy, about as far as one could get from the Fondor system without venturing into the Corporate sector. To Anakin, the droids were further evidence that the derelict had not come straight from the Unknown Regions.

Each droid was armed with a flexisteel dueling saber. The door slid shut behind them.

"Hello," Anakin said, his voice slightly muffled by his helmet.

The Duelist Elites raised their sabers and jumped at Anakin. They were still in the air as Anakin's lightsaber blazed on and he swung at them, neatly cleaving their heads from their necks in a single motion. The decapitated droids clattered to the floor.

Anakin's defense had been pure reflex, but as he looked at the fallen droids, he realized that he had disposed of them too hastily. Both droids had vocabulators, which meant they might have been able to tell him how they had come to be in the derelict.

Anakin hoped he had not damaged the droids beyond repair. He picked up one of the severed heads and found two blue wires sticking out of the neck socket. After twisting the wires together, he pressed back a metal plate and switched on the droid's speech generator.

"*Iltci avmaa ewidthu*," rasped the droid's head.

Anakin made an adjustment to the Duelist Elite's communication module, then asked, "What did you say?"

"I am incapacitated," the droid answered in Basic.

"I'm searching for a Jedi Knight named Obi-Wan Kenobi and the crews of two missing freighters. Do you know where they are?"

The droid was silent.

"Is this transport the *Sun Runner*?"

"I know nothing," the droid stated.

"Well, what do you know? Who programmed you? Why are you here?" When the droid did not immediately respond, Anakin warned, "If you don't give me answers, I'll pry them out of your memory banks."

"Prying will not help," the droid replied. "We all had memory wipes. We do not know who programmed us to defend the transport."

Anakin tweaked another wire to dislodge any stored data, then asked, "Are there more droids on board?"

"Yes. An R1 astromech and three 501-Z security droids are in the control room."

"Is the R1 controlling the ship?"

"Yes," said the Duelist Elite.

"What's your destination?"

"Only the R1 knows."

"Have you ever heard of Nallastia or the Fondor system?"

"If I did," the droid stated, "it was before my memory wipe."

Anakin asked, "How do I get to the control room?"

"There's an access tunnel on the other side of the door I came through. It leads to the control room."

The droid's illuminated optic visor flickered. Anakin knew the droid's battery was draining fast. "Are there any captives on board?"

"In a hangar that adjoins the control room," the droid answered. "We used a tractor beam to capture their ships. They are—" Before the Duelist Elite could complete his statement, his visor dimmed and went black.

Anakin tossed the metal head aside and headed for the door to the access passage.

CHAPTER EIGHT

It took Anakin less than a minute to use his lightsaber to carve an opening through the metal door. After he deactivated his weapon, he stepped through the opening and into the access passage, a long tunnel that vanished into darkness.

Darkness. Without even the light of distant stars to illuminate the passage, he was reminded of a recent dream in which he had been lost in a sea of black space, unable to find his way out. Anakin closed his eyes and concentrated, trying to rid himself of the bad memory and focus on his mission.

When Anakin opened his eyes, his vision had adjusted to the passage interior. To his left, an industrial gravsled hovered a few centimeters above the floor. The Duelist Elite had not told him about the gravsled, but Anakin decided to use it.

He climbed and felt for the controls. He found the lights and ignition, then started the repulsorlift engine. The gravsled blasted forward through the passage, and Anakin kept his head low, careful not to let his helmet smack against the passage's ceiling.

Seconds later, the end of the passage came into view. Anakin killed the ignition and let the gravsled slide to a silent stop. Stepping off the vehicle, he braced his body against the passage wall and clung to the shadows. Edging forward, he peered into the ship's control room. It had an even higher ceiling than the previous chamber, and Anakin could clearly see the cross beams and struts that supported the ship's superstructure, including the inner hull plating. The interior was dominated by a large orb-shaped hypermatter reactor, the ship's energy source. The control room was also filled with exotic navigational equipment, including what appeared to be a sensor jammer. The hypermatter reactor and all of the navigational equipment were contemporary, and the exposed inner hull had been assembled from new materials. Anakin now knew that the ship, despite its exterior's appearance, was not the ancient *Sun Runner*. It was a replica of some sort.

A magnet crane, used to move heavy equipment within the chamber, was suspended from a ceiling-mounted track. There were no viewports, but a wide monitor displayed a view of a distant crescent that was surrounded by smaller lights. Anakin recognized the crescent as Fondor, and the smaller lights as the orbital starship yards.

The so-called "derelict" was heading straight for Fondor.

To Anakin's left, near the wide monitor, a tall, dome-headed, black R1 astromech droid stood with one of its manipulator arms jacked into a tech station. Also visible were a pair of heavily armed 501-Z police droids, who stood at attention near an open hatch. Remembering the information he gained from the Duelist Elite, Anakin believed the open hatch led to the vessel's concealed hangar.

Neither the R1 nor the two 501-Zs were looking in Anakin's direction. Moving cautiously, Anakin stepped out of the tunnel and into the control room, only to hear a digitized voice order, "Halt!"

The voice came from Anakin's right, and he turned to see a third 501-Z security droid staring at him through the optical slot in its durasteel head. Anakin instantly realized the 501-Z must have been just out of his visual range, braced against the wall outside the tunnel as it guarded the tunnel's entrance. As the 501-Z had already loosened its blaster rifle and was aiming it at Anakin's head, Anakin gave the droid his undivided attention.

Anakin dropped to a crouch as the 501-Z fired at where Anakin's head had just been. As Anakin felt the discharged energy bolt speed over him, he raised his hand so that his palm faced his attacker and used the Force to hurl the 501-Z across the chamber. The droid smashed against the metal wall with an incredible impact, leaving a deep dent as it fell to the floor.

Less than two seconds had passed from the 501-Z's order of "Halt!" to its destruction. In that time, the two other 501-Zs assumed attack position and the tall R1 astromech, still jacked into the tech station, rotated its domed head to gaze at the human intruder.

As both remaining 501-Zs lurched forward, Anakin noticed they had moved directly under the magnet crane. He spotted the crane's controls just as the droids drew their blaster rifles. The droids were about to fire when Anakin reached out with the Force to activate the crane. In a blink, the 501-Zs lifted from the floor and slammed against the looming crane.

Anakin turned for the R1, which let out a nervous, electronic squeal before its lights went dead. Anakin realized the R1's systems had completely shut down. He rushed to the tech station and examined a datascreen. According to the data, the massive vessel would reach Fondor in twelve minutes, and the navicomputer was locked out. There was no way to adjust the guidance controls or alter the vessel's course and speed.

Besides the door to the access tunnel, there was only a single open hatch in the control room. Anakin hoped the Duelist Elite had not been lying about the adjoining hangar. If the hangar was not there, Anakin had no idea where to begin looking for Obi-Wan and the other captives on the inexact replica of the *Sun Runner*. But he did know that he had less than twelve minutes to stop the massive ship from reaching Fondor, and there was only one way to stop it.

It had to be destroyed.

Anakin ran for the open hatch.

CHAPTER NINE

The Duelist Elite had not lied. The control room's open hatch led directly into a pressurized hangar where Anakin found the Nallastian freighter, the Fondor Space Patrol ship, and Obi-Wan's Z-95 Headhunter.

Anakin saw his Master seated within the Head-hunter's cockpit. Like Anakin, Obi-Wan still wore a g-suit. Anakin ran toward the starfighter, but stopped short as he smacked into an invisible barrier.

It was a force field. Anakin now saw that the hangar's tractor-beam projector was trained on all three ships, immobilizing them on the hangar floor. Anakin activated his lightsaber and leaped at the projector, sweeping his weapon's blade through the device. Sparks erupted from the ruined projec-tor, and the force field dropped, freeing the three ships.

The crews of the freighter and the space patrol ship wasted no time in making their escape. Both ships fired their engines and launched—much to Anakin's surprise—through what appeared to be one of the hangar's wide metal walls.

Obi-Wan raised the Headhunter's cockpit canopy, looked at Anakin, and said, "You were sup-posed to stay on my wing."

"Forgive me, Master," Anakin quickly replied, "but I've learned that this vessel isn't really the

Sun Runner, and that it's heading straight for Fondor. The guidance controls are locked, and we only have about eleven minutes. I think we must destroy the ship. The control room is beyond that hatch, and there's a hypermatter reactor. We just need some explosives."

"Sounds like you've been busy," Obi-Wan said as he scrambled out of the cockpit. "Good thing you *didn't* stay on my wing, or both of us might have been captured."

Anakin pointed at the wall through which the freighter and patrol ship had departed. "The wall is a hologram?"

"It conceals the docking port," Obi-Wan answered as he opened his fighter's compact cargo bay. "From space, the hologram looks like hull plating. The tractor beam snagged my fighter and dragged me in, same as it did the other ships." From the fighter's cargo bay, Obi-Wan removed a proton grenade. He commented, "Senator Rodd certainly keeps his starfighters well supplied."

A terrible realization suddenly hit Anakin. "Master, your starfighter's cockpit is only large enough for one of us."

"I'm aware of that," Obi-Wan said as he handed the grenade to Anakin. "Since you know where to find the hypermatter reactor, you'll plant the grenade. We don't want this ship blowing up too close to Fondor, so set the timer for two minutes. I'll ready the Headhunter for launch, and you'll ride it out. Where's your starfighter?"

"Anchored near the missile silo."

"I'll carry you to it so you can make your own way back to the *Unitive*, instead of clinging to the outside of my ship like a mynock. Go, now."

Carrying the grenade, Anakin ran for the hatch that led to the control room while Obi-Wan climbed back into the Headhunter's cockpit. Inside the control room, Anakin twisted the grenade's arming mechanism, priming a battery to deliver a small electrical charge to the weapon's proton core. Then he pressed the grenade's activation plunger, planted the grenade against the hypermatter reactor, and ran back through the hatch.

Returning to the concealed hangar, Anakin saw that the Headhunter was angled straight for the holographic hull plate that concealed the hangar's port. He made sure his insulated helmet was still sealed tightly to the neck of his g-suit, then sprang for the Headhunter and gripped the handle on the cargo bay.

Carrying Anakin, the Headhunter lifted from the hangar floor, then launched toward the hologram-hidden port. Obi-Wan piloted the starfighter through the hologram, out of the port, and then looped back around the massive ship's cylindrical exterior until he arrived at the ruined missile silo, where Anakin's CloakShape remained anchored. They were all still speeding toward Fondor and its starship yards.

Obi-Wan closed the distance between the Headhunter and the anchored CloakShape, and Anakin stretched his legs out to his waiting starfighter. The moment Anakin's boots contacted the CloakShape's hull, he released his grip on the Headhunter's cargo hold. Obi-Wan kept the Headhunter close to the CloakShape while he watched Anakin pop his starfighter's canopy and enter the cockpit. As soon as Anakin was safely behind the controls, Obi-Wan guided his Headhunter away.

Following his Master's lead, Anakin released the CloakShape from the larger ship's hull and sped after the Headhunter. He sighted Obi-Wan's fighter in front of him and tried using his starship's comm to hail the other fighter, but the comm only produced a dead signal. Anakin remembered the sensor jammer he had seen in the mysterious ship's control room and he realized the jammer was still operating. But not for long.

Behind Anakin, the massive ship was suddenly wracked by a tremendous explosion. The shock wave sent metal debris in all directions, as far out as Anakin's starfighter. The CloakShape's particle shields held up against the hammering rain of debris, but the shock wave knocked the starfighter off course, separating Anakin from Obi-Wan even more.

Anakin gripped the CloakShape's controls and reoriented himself, then looked back at the site of the explosion. Although most of the ship had been reduced to small bits, a large, cylindrical fragment remained intact. To Anakin, it looked like a gigantic cross section. The giant hunk of wreckage hurtled away from the explosion. As best as Anakin could see, it was on a collision course for Fondor's moon, Nallastia.

The only thing Anakin really knew about Nallastia was that it was a jungle world. He imagined the effect of flaming wreckage, crashing down through the moon's atmosphere to the forests below. He knew he could not let that happen.

Still unable to contact Obi-Wan, Anakin steered after the wreckage, accelerating past the smaller debris. As he neared the wreckage, he spotted a dark blemish on a surface area and he realized he was looking at the scorched remains of the concealed missile silo. Evidently, the explosion in the ship's control room failed to travel all the way through the tunnel to the chamber beside the missile silo.

Which meant the rack of eighteen highly explosive missiles was still intact.

Anakin remembered the cracked wall in the chamber that contained the racked missiles. He aimed the CloakShape's concussion-missile launcher at the missile silo and fired.

High over the moon Nallastia, the giant piece of wreckage exploded into billions of particles, most no larger than grains of sand. Unfortunately, Anakin had not been able to put much distance between himself and the explosion, and the CloakShape caught most of the shock wave. The starfighter was tossed like a flimsy toy, sending Anakin into an out-of-control spiral, down through Nallastia's atmosphere.

Gazing through his cockpit canopy, Anakin tried to see Nallastia's surface, but all he could make out was a rapidly swirling blur of darkness. He was descending upon the side of the moon that was currently cast in shadow, facing away from the sun. As he struggled to gain control of the CloakShape, he knew the Nallastian night would soon be illuminated by his starfighter's fiery crash.

So Anakin ejected. Explosive bolts released his starfighter's canopy, and his seat blasted out of the cockpit. As the seat's automatic landing jets carried Anakin down to Nallastia, he watched as the CloakShape spiraled nosefirst into a grassy field, then blossom into a burst of flame.

Under the night sky, Anakin steered his ejected seat down near the CloakShape's crash site. All he could do now was try to extinguish the flames. With his starfighter destroyed, he had no means of leaving Nallastia or contacting the *Unitive*.

He wondered how long it would take for Obi-Wan to find him.

CHAPTER TEN

At this point, readers who chose to follow the adventure in the *Star Wars* Adventures Game Book can return to *Hunt the Sun Runner*.

"Anakin?" Obi-Wan repeated into his starfighter's comm. "Anakin, do you read me?"

Obi-Wan had lost sight of Anakin after the first explosion decimated the mysterious derelict. Afterward, he had seen a second explosion near the moon Nallastia, but he did not know whether Anakin had anything to do with it. Even though the replica of the *Sun Runner* and its sensor-jamming equipment were now destroyed, Obi Wan could not seem to get a clear signal on any transceiver frequencies. He suspected all the exploded debris was causing the interference.

Obi-Wan searched the starscape with his eyes, trying to find any trace of Anakin's CloakShape. Several minutes later, Obi-Wan noticed that his Headhunter's fuel gauge was showing an alarmingly low level of energy. A quick calculation confirmed he would have just enough fuel to reach Fondor, where he could refuel before returning to the *Unitive*. He would have to wait until later to resume his search for Anakin.

As Obi-Wan angled his starfighter toward Fondor's starship yards, he found himself thinking about his hasty conversation with Anakin in the mammoth ship's hangar. Anakin had said he discovered the ship was not the *Sun Runner*, which did not surprise Obi-Wan, who had been suspicious of the derelict from the start. But as he considered the fact that the derelict had been an elaborate counterfeit, he wondered who would have built what must have been an expensive replica of the *Sun Runner*, and then aimed it at Fondor.

Obi-Wan knew the questions would nag at him until he learned the truth.

* * *

On the planet Esseles in the Darpa sector, far from the Fondor system, a Hutt named Groodo lived in a palace in the capital city of Calamar. Groodo had many pleasures, but revenge was at the top of his list. Nothing made him happier than taking vengeance on anyone who was fool enough to wrong him. Groodo even found himself looking forward to being wronged, just so he would have the opportunity to get even.

Besides plotting vengeful acts, Groodo had his business interests. For many years, he had run a factory on Esseles, specializing in the manufacture of customized hyperdrive engines. He still owned the factory, but had turned its operations over to his son, Boonda. Groodo now dedicated most of his energy to the development of Groodo

Starship Yards, which orbited Esseles. He was in his den, admiring a holographic model of a Republic Sienar Systems Marauder-class corvette, when his Boonda slithered into the room.

"Greetings, my ignorant spawn," Groodo drawled.

Boonda chuckled. His father often called him by that term of affection. "Hi, Pop," Boonda said cheerfully. "Sorry to bother you, but do you remember that secret replica job at your starship yards?"

"Of course, I remember it, you hopeless sack of fat," Groodo replied. "It's a four-hundred-meter-long Corellia StarDrive Alpha-class heavy transport, deliberately distressed to look like it's four thousand years old, and it bears the markings of the *Sun Runner*."

"Yeah, that's the one I meant," Boonda said. "Did you know it's been stolen from your starship yard?"

"*Stolen*?" Groodo said, rolling his eyes in disbelief. "Quick! Call the insurance company!"

While Boonda slithered out of the den to contact the insurers, a twisted smile crept across Groodo's face. He knew for a fact that the duplicate of the *Sun Runner* had not been stolen. He had rigged the ship's hyperdrive himself and he knew it had gone all the way to the Fondor system, carrying his memory-wiped droids with it. It was all part of his latest and most elaborate plan for revenge. The way he had it figured, the starship yards of Fondor would be out of business within a week. Then their business would be his. That would show those spineless would-be industrialists not to underestimate him again.

Groodo returned his attention to the hologram of the Marauder corvette and began to whistle.

* * *

Back in the Fondor system, on the moon Nallastia, Anakin was nearly exhausted by the time he extinguished most of the burning wreckage from his crashed CloakShape. His only consolation was that he had prevented a greater disaster. If he had not destroyed the mysterious ship's largest remnant in space, many square kilometers of Nallastian jungle would have burned to the ground. It was pure luck that his starfighter had not crashed in a populated area.

Anakin prepared to dig in for the night. After removing his helmet and the outer layer of his g-suit, he dragged the remaining burning wreckage to a safe location and constructed a campfire, which he hoped might help Obi-Wan find him. Then he wondered if he were anywhere near a Nallastian village, and if the Nallastians would find him first.

He used his lightsaber to cut several broad, flexible leaves from a tree and assembled the leaves into a shelter at the tree's base. He was more than ready to go to sleep. He only wished he wouldn't have any more bad dreams.

Anakin removed his boots and belt and placed them in the shelter. He was about to slip into the shelter himself when he heard something snap. The sound did not come from the nearby campfire, but from the shadows between a group of nearby trees.

Anakin stepped closer to the campfire, keeping his back to the flames; and he gazed out into the darkness. A low growl rumbled from the nearby trees, and he saw a pair of menacing yellow eyes open and stare back at him. Based on the distance between the two eyes, he guessed the creature's head was quite large.

Anakin reached for his lightsaber, but it was not where it should have been. He forgot that he had left it clipped to his belt, which was now resting inside the shelter of broad leaves.

The yellow-eyed creature growled again, then leaped from the shadows.

NEXT ADVENTURE:
THE CAVERN OF SCREAMING SKULLS